Buddy

ELLEN MILES

■ SCHOLASTIC

For Barley, Ursa, Jack, Allie, Chico,

and all the other mutts I've known and loved.

Scholastic Children's Books
An imprint of Scholastic Ltd
Euston House, 24 Eversholt Street
London, NW1 1DB, UK
Registered office: Westfield Road, Southam, Warwickshire, CV47 0RA
SCHOLASTIC and associated logos are trademarks and or registered trademarks of
Scholastic Inc.

First published in the US by Scholastic Inc., 2007
This edition published in the UK by Scholastic Ltd, 2007

Text copyright © Ellen Miles, 2007

The right of Ellen Miles to be identified as the author of this work
has been asserted by her.

10 digit ISBN 1 407 10335 0
13 digit ISBN 978 1407 10335 8

British Library Cataloguing-in-Publication Data.
A CIP catalogue record for this book is available from the British Library

Printed in the UK by CPI Bookmarque, Croydon, CR0 4TD
Papers used by Scholastic Children's Books are made from wood grown in
sustainable forests.

9 10 8

www.scholastic.co.uk/zone

CHapter ONe

Lizzie Peterson pushed open the door of Caring Paws, the animal shelter where she volunteered.

"Lizzie! Is it already three o'clock?" The director, Ms Dobbins, looked tired and distracted. "We have been so busy here today!"

"Actually, it's only two-thirty," Lizzie said. "I'm a little early." She wrote her name on the volunteer sign-in sheet and checked the wipe-off board for new names. "Who's Skipper?" she asked when she saw the name written in red, the colour for dogs. "And what does that mean, Skipper and Company?"

It was always exciting when a new animal arrived at the shelter. Maybe one of the new dogs would be her family's next foster puppy! Lizzie had been volunteering at Caring Paws for two months. She came every Saturday afternoon. She loved being around all the dogs and cats and the people who cared for them.

Caring Paws was a place for animals that needed homes. Some were strays who had been found on country roads or in car parks. The shelter staff tried hard to find their owners. Other cats or dogs had been abandoned, left near a farm or on someone's porch. And some were beloved pets that the owners had to give up.

Ms Dobbins did her best to help find the perfect home for every animal that came to Caring Paws. But while they waited to find their forever families, the animals needed exercise, love and care. That was where the volunteers came in. There was always work to do: answering the phone, cleaning cages, feeding animals, giving them baths. Because Lizzie was only in Year Four, she didn't do any of those jobs. She got to do the best job of all: exercising the dogs!

Lizzie was mad about dogs. She loved to play with them, read about them, make up stories about them, and learn everything she could about them. She and her younger brother Jack wanted their own dog more than anything, and they had been bugging their parents about it for years. Lizzie's dad loved dogs, too – but Mum was more of a cat person. So far, both parents agreed that the family was not ready for a full-time dog.

That was partly because of Lizzie's other brother, the Bean. (His real name was Adam, but nobody ever called him that.) He was just a toddler, and keeping him out of trouble took up a lot of everyone's energy. The funny thing was that the Bean loved dogs, too. He loved them so much that he liked to pretend he was one. He crawled around during mealtimes, barked at visitors, and played with dog toys more than kid toys.

"The Bean is enough dog for now," Mum always said. She liked to point out that the Bean did not shed fur all over the place, make messes, or chew up their shoes, the way a real dog would.

For now, Lizzie and Jack had to be happy with part-time puppies. The Petersons had become a foster family, taking care of puppies until the perfect home could be found for each one. So far, they had fostered four different puppies.

Goldie, the first puppy, was a happy golden retriever who had belonged to a family whose house had burned down. Mr Peterson was a fireman, and he brought her home after putting out the fire. Goldie ended up living next door with Sammy, Jack's best friend. She was the perfect pal for Sammy's older dog, Rufus.

The next pup was Snowball, a fluffy little West Highland white terrier. He had a lot of energy and a big, big personality. The Petersons found Snowball an excellent home with a nice lady named Mrs Peabody.

Shadow, the serious black Lab puppy, came next. With help from Maria, her new best friend, Lizzie found him a home with a family that would train him to be a guide dog for a blind person.

Then there was Rascal, the wild child. He was an energetic Jack Russell terrier who could not learn to behave well enough to live with a regular family in a regular house. Rascal had ended up living at a riding stable, where he didn't need to have "indoor manners". It was the perfect home for a rascally dog.

Lizzie, Jack and the Bean had loved every one of those puppies. They had hoped and wished that they would be able to keep each one themselves. But they knew that the puppies had found just the right homes, and that was the most important thing.

It had been quite a while since the Petersons had fostered a puppy. That was why Lizzie had started volunteering at Caring Paws in the first place. She missed being around dogs!

Now, at the shelter, Lizzie could hardly wait to

meet the newest dog, Skipper. "Is Skipper a boy or a girl?" she asked Ms Dobbins.

Ms Dobbins paused. "She's a girl," she answered after a moment. "And here's the thing. We are so full right now that I just don't know where I'm going to put her! I've already got two dogs doubled up in kennel five. We have more than a dozen dogs looking for homes! There is just no room here – and Skipper really, really needs more space to be comfortable. We need a foster family for her."

"Maybe my family can take her," Lizzie suggested. "Is Skipper a puppy?"

"Well . . . no," said Ms Dobbins. "But—"

"It doesn't matter," Lizzie interrupted. "If she needs a home, and there's no room here, I'm sure we can take care of her for a while. I'll just have to convince my mum. She's used to fostering puppies, so talking her into a dog should be a breeze."

As they were talking, Ms Dobbins was leading the way down the hall to the dog room. She and Lizzie walked past the exam room, where a visiting vet checked out every animal that came into the shelter. They passed the tub room, the scene of many soapy, hairy messes. And then there were the two cat rooms Lizzie peeked in. She could see all kinds of cats and kittens. They were napping and climbing and cleaning themselves.

As they approached the dog room, Lizzie could hear dogs barking. It was funny. Sometimes only one dog was barking in the dog room. But other times, all the dogs started barking at once, as if they were kids in a classroom yelling, "Call on me! Call on me!"

Ms Dobbins pushed open the door to the dog room. Inside, there were ten kennels made of metal fencing that stretched from the floor to the ceiling. Each kennel had a comfy bed, a sign on the outside with the dog's name, and directions about feeding and walking. Each kennel also had a doggie door that could open to a fenced area outdoors, so the dogs could get outside on their own when there wasn't a volunteer to walk them. The room was warm and bright, and there were hand-painted number signs for each kennel. Lizzie knew that animal shelters could be sad places, and she was glad that Caring Paws always seemed cheerful and homey.

Ms Dobbins pointed at kennel number one, the cage nearest the door. "That's Skipper," she said. "And now you know what 'and company' means."

There, in the kennel, was a brown and tan dog with a silky-soft coat. Her big cocoa-brown eyes were shiny, and she had ears that stood straight up. Right now they were pointed towards the door, as if Skipper had radar. But Skipper didn't jump to her feet, the way most dogs did when you came into the kennels. She just stayed where she was, looking up at Ms Dobbins.

*   *   *

Skipper wondered who the new person was. Could she trust her? Should she stand up and show off her treasure? She decided it was safe.

When Skipper moved, Lizzie gasped. "Oh, my!" she said when she saw what was curled up in the curve of Skipper's belly.

Three puppies.

Three tiny, adorable, brown and tan puppies, and they were just beginning to squirm themselves awake.

Chapter Two

For a minute, Lizzie couldn't say anything. She just stared. "Ohh," she finally sighed. "They are so, so cute!"

The puppies had fluffy, soft-looking coats. Two of them were mostly brown with tan markings. One of those puppies was a darker brown, and one was lighter. They were both larger than the third puppy, who was mostly tan with brown markings. All three looked sleepy and cosy, curled up near their mother. One of them yawned as Lizzie was watching, and she could see its curly pink tongue. Another one got up and tottered away from its mother on unsteady legs. Its tiny tail stuck straight up in the air. Lizzie knew her brother Jack would love these puppies.

"The two bigger ones are girls," said Ms Dobbins. "And the little tan one is a boy. See the heart on his chest?"

Just then, the tan pup climbed over one of his sisters, and Lizzie spotted the white marking Ms Dobbins was talking about. "They look like they might be part German shepherd," she said. "Or maybe chow?"

Lizzie had a "Dog Breeds of the World" poster in her room at home. She loved to study it and learn about every kind of dog. Usually she could tell right away what breed of dog she was looking at, but Skipper and her puppies looked like they were a mix of breeds. "All-American dogs," her poster called them. "Mutts," her dad always said. He said mixed-breed dogs were the best.

Ms Dobbins agreed. She had told Lizzie that mutts often combined the best things about each breed, creating a new kind of dog that was good-looking, healthy and strong. For example, if a dog's father was a Labrador retriever and its mother was a collie, you might get a puppy that was great with kids and liked to fetch balls (like a Lab) and was also loyal and had a soft, silky coat (like a collie).

"We haven't quite figured out what mix these puppies are," said Ms Dobbins. "They may have some golden retriever in them, too. They're so friendly and sweet!"

"What are their names?" asked Lizzie.

Ms Dobbins shrugged. "It's been so crazy around here, I haven't had a chance to name the puppies," she answered. "Julie named the mother Skipper, but we figured that whoever adopts the pups should get to name them."

Lizzie liked Julie. She was a senior in high school who worked at the shelter. Lizzie thought Julie was the coolest. She seemed to know everything about dogs and cats. Plus, she was always coming up with great ideas for making the shelter work better – like the colour-coded wipe-off board.

Lizzie stared at Skipper's family. The puppies were making soft whimpering and snuffling noises as they pushed towards their mother, getting ready to nurse. "How old are they?" she asked.

"We think they're four or five weeks old," said Ms Dobbins. "They have their eyes open, and they can walk and even run around a bit. So they aren't too young. But they still need their mother. They're just about ready to start eating solid food, but they're not quite ready to be on their own."

"So that means—" Lizzie was just beginning to figure it out.

Ms Dobbins nodded. "I think you get the picture," she said. "Whoever fosters Skipper takes the puppies, too. The whole litter. It's a package deal. And not one that everybody is ready for. It's a lot of responsibility."

"I know," Lizzie said. "Jack and I have taken care of lots of puppies. One puppy at a time is plenty. Three puppies and a mum . . . wow."

"Not only that," said Ms Dobbins, "but there's a time commitment, too. If someone takes these puppies, they're going to have to keep them until they're old enough to go to their real homes."

"Like, until they're eight weeks old?" Lizzie asked. She had learned a lot about puppies.

"That's right," said Ms Dobbins.

Lizzie nodded. It wouldn't be easy to talk her mother into fostering Skipper and the puppies, especially for three or four whole weeks. But Lizzie was sure that the Petersons were the perfect family to take them in. She had already fallen completely in love with the puppies, and she knew she and her family could give them all the care they needed. "Where did they come from?" she asked.

Ms Dobbins sighed. "A policeman found them living in back of the supermarket, near the bins. Skipper had made a nest out of old cardboard boxes, and she was getting by on whatever food she could find in the rubbish. She did her best, but it wasn't easy taking care of her pups under those conditions."

Lizzie felt tears spring into her eyes just thinking about it. "That's so sad," she said. She hated to imagine how a sweet dog like Skipper could have ended up living in a car park.

"Skipper's puppies are pretty wonderful, too," said Ms Dobbins. "When the policemen found the puppies, Skipper was off finding food. The two girl puppies were huddled around the little boy puppy, keeping him warm. They are the best kind of big sisters."

The whole time Lizzie and Ms Dobbins had been talking, a dog had been barking like crazy. Now, suddenly, all the rest of the dogs decided they needed to bark, too. The noise filled the dog room, bouncing off the concrete floors and walls. The only dog who wasn't barking was Skipper. She was nuzzling her puppies while they nursed. She seemed calm and content, even in the midst of all that noise.

Ms Dobbins smiled at Lizzie and shook her head. "What a racket!" she yelled. "Let's go back to the office and talk where we can hear each other."

Lizzie took one more look at Skipper and her puppies. She felt her throat close up as if she were about to cry. Skipper had done everything she could to take care of her family. She deserved a break. She deserved some help.

"Can I call my mum?" Lizzie asked as soon as she and Ms Dobbins walked into the office. A dog and three puppies. This was a big deal! Skipper needed the Petersons' help. Lizzie needed to talk to her family.

Ms Dobbins nodded towards the phone. "Go right ahead," she said.

Lizzie dialled her number and crossed her fingers while the phone rang. When her mother said hello, Lizzie said, "Mum? It's me. Lizzie. You'll never believe it, but there's a dog here I think we should foster."

"A dog?" her mum asked. "Not a puppy?"

"Well . . ." said Lizzie. "Can you come down here – and bring Dad and Jack and the Bean, too? I think it's time for a Peterson Powwow."

Chapter Three

When Lizzie hung up, Ms Dobbins was giving her a curious look. "A Peterson Powwow?" she asked.

Lizzie nodded. "It's a special meeting," she said. "We always have one for really important family decisions." It wasn't always easy to get all the Petersons together, but when somebody mentioned a powwow, they would drop everything else to attend.

"Well," said Ms Dobbins. "This is definitely a really important decision. Taking Skipper and her pups would be a big responsibility, and your whole family has to agree that it's the right thing to do."

Lizzie nodded again. "I know," she said. She could guess exactly how each member of her family would feel about fostering Skipper and the three puppies. Jack would be all for it. So would the Bean, of course. Dad would be concerned, but he would agree to it, as long as Lizzie and Jack promised that they would do most of the work. And Mum? She would definitely need some convincing. Mum had got used to the idea of the family fostering puppies, but so far they had only taken one at a time. This was a whole different story.

Lizzie walked three shelter dogs while she waited for her family to arrive. She kept her fingers crossed the whole time.

She kept checking on Skipper and her pups, too. By the third time Lizzie visited, she was pretty sure that Skipper recognized her. And she was definitely sure that Skipper liked her. Some dog mothers could be very protective, but Lizzie thought Skipper would trust her around the puppies. She could hardly wait to hold them in her lap!

Finally, when she was out in the fenced-in yard playing fetch with a black Lab named Tigger, she saw her dad's red pickup pull into the car park.

Lizzie ran inside and put Tigger back in his kennel, just as Ms Dobbins came into the dog room, followed by Jack, Dad and Mum. Dad had the Bean by the hand, holding him tightly so that he wouldn't run up to each of the kennels and put his fingers through the wire. Dogs and puppies always seemed to love the Bean, but Lizzie and her family knew it was best to play it safe.

Mum had her hands over her ears. All the dogs were barking to greet the new visitors, and the dog room was pretty noisy.

"Lizzie?" asked Ms Dobbins. "Would you like to introduce your family to Skipper?"

Lizzie's heart thumped. More than anything, she wanted to take Skipper home with them, and help her keep her babies safe and warm and happy until they could find perfect homes for each one. By now, she'd had her fingers crossed for so long that they were feeling cramped. But she tried to hide the nervousness in her voice. "Sure," she said. "She's over here." She led the way to Skipper's kennel.

Skipper was curled up on a green corduroy dog bed with a proud, motherly look on her pretty brown-and-tan face. Her three puppies gave squeaky barks and growls as they crawled around busily, climbing over one another in a big, happy puppy pile.

Lizzie looked at her mum hopefully as the family approached the kennel. "You see," she began, "the thing is that Skipper has—"

Jack saw them first. "Puppies!" He gasped in surprise.

When Dad saw them, he let out a "Whoa!" But he had a big smile on his face.

"Uppy!" yelled the Bean, laughing his googly laugh.

Mum took one look and turned to Lizzie. "Elizabeth Maude Peterson," she said. "Are you out of your mind?" She only used Lizzie's full name when she was really, really upset with her.

"Mum—" Lizzie began.

Ms Dobbins interrupted. "I know it's a lot to ask," she said. "And normally, I would only send Skipper and her family to a home where the caretakers were experienced with very young puppies. But we're in a jam. We just have too many dogs on our hands."

Dad and Jack and the Bean were talking excitedly as they watched the puppies play.

"Look at that little one," said Dad. "What a cutie!"

"That's the boy," Lizzie told him. "The other two are girls."

"Bossy big sisters," said Jack. "Just like mine." He grinned and stuck out his tongue at Lizzie. Meanwhile, the two bigger puppies knocked the smaller one down as they wrestled over a squeaky rubber toy. Jack laughed. "They look just like the puppies in that book *So Many Puppies,*" he said. That was one of his and Lizzie's favourite books of all time. Mary Thompson, the author, had just moved to Littleton. That was big news. And there was even bigger news: on Monday she was coming to Littleton Primary to meet all the classes!

Jack and Lizzie's mum, who was a reporter for the *Littleton News*, had written an article about the author. She had gone to her house to interview her, and she said Mary Thompson wasn't stuck up at all, even though she was famous.

Now Mrs Peterson didn't say a word. She wasn't even watching the puppies. She was still frowning at Lizzie. "How could we possibly handle a whole litter of puppies?" she asked. "With you and Jack in school, and the Bean needing so much attention at home?" She shook her head.

"Oh, Mum," said Jack. "Please? Pretty please?" He looked at her pleadingly.

"Uppy?" Bean asked hopefully.

"OK, powwow time," Dad said. "Here's what I think: It would be a lot of work, but if we all pitch in, we can do it." He smiled down at Lizzie and Jack. "These two have proved that they can be very responsible," he reminded Mum. "I'm game if the rest of you are," he finished.

"It would be a great family experience," Lizzie added. She knew her mother was big on things that brought the family together. "And it's only for a few weeks."

"And you'd be doing us a *huge* favour," said Ms Dobbins. "We will support you in any way we can, including giving you supplies and plenty of advice."

Mum finally stopped staring at Lizzie. She glanced into the kennel at Skipper and her puppies, and Lizzie saw her mum's eyes soften. The boy puppy was whimpering for his mother. He needed help. He was stuck between two big dog bowls. Skipper nudged him gently, and his whimpers turned to happy sighs as he ran away from the bowls and to his Mum's side.

Lizzie had the feeling that her mum was beginning to feel a connection to Skipper. After all, they were both mothers. "Mum?" Lizzie asked softly. "Please?"

"Well. . ." Mum said.

Chapter Four

Jack woke up early the next morning. As soon as he opened his eyes, he remembered: puppies! He threw a sweater over his pyjamas and went downstairs, thankful that it was Sunday and he could spend the whole day at home with Skipper and her three babies. The house was quiet. When he turned on the light in the kitchen, Skipper looked up at him with her soft brown eyes.

Jack felt lucky to be the first one up. It gave him a chance to be alone with the puppies. Things had been so crazy the night before! He had not had the chance to really get to know them.

Once the whole family had agreed to foster Skipper and her puppies, things had moved very fast. After a crash course in puppy-raising from

Ms Dobbins, the Petersons had brought the whole gang home that very night.

Before dinner, Dad had gone into town and brought back a big box that had once held a washing machine. He also brought home egg rolls and chicken lo mein from China Star. That was Jack's favourite dinner, next to pizza.

Before they sat down to eat, Jack, Lizzie and Dad cut up the big box and put it in a corner of the kitchen. Once they had made an opening for a door, it made a perfect bed for Skipper and her puppies. The Bean donated one of his old baby blankets and two of his favourite dog toys: his fluffy sheepskin Dolly, and the long, tattered Snakey.

It took the rest of the evening to get Skipper and her puppies settled in, and by bedtime Jack and Lizzie were exhausted. Even the Bean crawled into his "big-boy bed" without any of his usual tricks. Mum and Dad promised to check on the puppies at least once in the middle of the night.

Now, in the early-morning light of the kitchen, Skipper lifted her head and thumped her tail when Jack approached the box. "Good girl," said Jack, patting Skipper's silky ears.

The three puppies were deep in sleep, but they began to stir when they heard Jack. Jack reached into the box to pick up the darker brown girl puppy. "It's OK, Skipper," he told the mother dog. "Ms Dobbins said it's time to start letting the pups get used to people. I promise to be very, very careful."

Skipper knew she could trust the boy. He was gentle and kind. But it wasn't easy to see her puppy so far away. She whimpered softly and watched very closely as the boy put the puppy on his lap.

Jack sat cross-legged on the kitchen floor, cuddling the soft, warm, squirmy pup.

"You're up early," said Dad when he came into

the kitchen a few minutes later. He got the coffee machine going, then knelt to pat Skipper. Lizzie arrived next, and soon she was sitting on the floor near Jack, holding the light brown girl puppy.

By the time everyone was downstairs, the kitchen was warm and bright and full of good smells as Dad flipped pancakes at the stove. Skipper was already beginning to get used to having people touch her puppies, and Jack and Lizzie were getting to know their new guests.

"Uppy!" said the Bean, running over to reach for a puppy.

"No, no," said Mum, catching him by the shirt.

"No" was not the Bean's favourite word. He stared up at Mum.

"You can look, and you can pet a puppy if Jack or Lizzie is holding it," Mum told him. "But the puppies are still very little, and we have to be very careful with them."

The Bean looked like he might start wailing.

"Sit here," Jack said quickly, patting the floor

beside him. "Watch! The puppies are going to eat breakfast!" He and Lizzie had tucked their puppies back in the box with their mother. They had been whining, and Lizzie knew they must be hungry. Sure enough, they ran straight to Skipper and began to nurse.

The puppies were so interesting to watch that the Petersons forgot all about their own breakfast. The pancakes sat on the table, getting cold.

"What about the little boy?" Mum asked after a while. "He's not getting anything to eat."

"That's because his stupid big sisters always push him out of the way," Jack said.

Gently, Mum reached into the box and helped the tan boy pup find a place to nurse. Then she patted Skipper on the head.

Skipper licked the nice lady's hand. She had a feeling the lady must be a mother, too. The lady knew that Skipper's little boy needed a little help.

*　　*　　*

"The boy puppy is very shy," said Lizzie.

"And the girl with the dark brown coat is really adventurous," Jack said. "She's always the first one to check out something new."

"The lighter one seems like a real lovebug," Dad noted. "She's full of kisses and she loves to be held."

It was amazing how each of the puppies had their own personalities, even though they were so young.

"We need to name them!" said Jack.

"Well, their forever families will probably want to do that," Mum said. She was always quick to remind Jack and Lizzie that they were only a foster family.

"Ms Dobbins said we could give them temporary names," Lizzie said. "I was thinking about Tic, Tac, and Toe."

"That's stupid!" Jack said. He had another idea. "I vote for Eenie, Meany, Miney and Moe!"

"But there are only three puppies!" Lizzie said.

Oops. That was true. Maybe he hadn't really thought those names through. But Jack didn't want to give up. "Right," he said. "Who would name a puppy Meany?"

Lizzie was just shaking her head.

"How about Larry, Moe and Curly?" asked Dad. "Those were the names of the Three Stooges, on TV. I used to love those guys." He gave Jack a tap on the head. "*Nyuk, nyuk, nyuk,*" he said in a funny voice.

Now Mum was shaking *her* head. "The Three Stooges were all boys," she reminded Dad. "I think we should name the puppies after their colours."

"What do you mean?" asked Lizzie.

"Well, we could call the light brown girl Cinnamon," Mum said.

Lizzie considered the name. "I like it," she said. She reached for the sweet girl puppy, who was extra drowsy after her nursing.

Jack liked it, too. Cinnamon toast was one of

his favourite snacks. "Yeah! And the darker brown one could be Cocoa!" he added. Her soft brown fur reminded him of hot chocolate, something he liked to drink when he was eating cinnamon toast.

"And what about you, buddy?!" Lizzie asked the little boy who was nosing around the box. "What's your name going to be?"

"How about . . . Buddy?" Jack asked. The name didn't have anything to do with the puppy's colour. But everybody noticed that the tiny boy looked up when Jack said the name. "He just seems like a little Buddy, you know?" The puppy looked up at Jack again.

"OK," said Lizzie, laughing. "Buddy it is."

"I think all the names are perfect," said Jack. He could not have felt happier. If there was anything more wonderful than fostering one puppy, it was fostering three!

Chapter Five

The Petersons' pancakes were still waiting on the table when Jack's best friend showed up.

"Where are the puppies?" Sammy asked as he barged into the kitchen that Sunday morning. "What's for breakfast? Is anyone going to eat those pancakes?" Sammy lived next door but he seemed to eat most of his meals at the Petersons'. He was always on time for breakfast, and he always burst in without knocking.

It was funny that Sammy didn't knock, because he loved telling knock-knock jokes. He had a new one almost every morning, and usually Jack had a joke to tell, too. But not this morning. Before Sammy could even say, "Knock-knock," Jack said,

"Shhh!" He pointed to the box. He had called Sammy the night before to tell him about the puppies. Now he couldn't wait to show them off, but he knew that it was best to be quiet around Skipper and her little ones.

Skipper was worried. Who was this loud new person? She got to her feet in case she would have to protect her puppies.

Cocoa wasn't scared at all. She started walking right towards the new boy. Everything new was interesting. Everything new was fun. Cocoa always wanted to find out more.

Cinnamon barely paid attention. She was too busy nuzzling the girl's chin. She would give her one more lick. OK. Maybe two.

Buddy wondered where his mother was going. Wait! He hadn't finished eating yet! He was so hungry. Why did his sisters always hog the food? They used to take care of him, but now they pushed him aside.

"Oh, wow," Sammy said in a hushed voice. "Boy, are they cute! Can I hold one?"

"Lap!" said the Bean sternly, pointing a finger at Sammy.

Everybody cracked up. "He knows the rules!" Lizzie said. "You have to be sitting on the floor to hold a puppy in your lap. They're just too squirmy for it to be safe any other way." Lizzie paused. "Oh, and watch out for their puppy teeth! They're just coming in, and they are super sharp. We'll have to start teaching them that it's not OK to bite."

Sammy was nodding. "OK, OK," he said, sitting down next to Jack. "Now can I hold one?"

Cocoa was already on her way over to check Sammy out. Jack helped him pick up the puppy so he could hold her in his lap. "This is Cocoa."

"And this is Cinnamon!" Lizzie smiled proudly down at the light brown puppy, who kept scrambling up to nibble on Lizzie's chin.

"And Buddy," said Jack, reaching out to stroke the tan boy puppy. Buddy was still waiting for

Skipper to settle down again, so he could eat some more. "He's shy."

"He's little, too," said Sammy. "And he's not running around like the others. What's wrong with him? Whoa there!" He held on to squirmy Cocoa, who was trying to wiggle away to go and look at something new.

"Nothing's wrong with him!" said Jack. But Buddy did seem slower than his sisters. Maybe he was just sleepy. After all, they had just eaten.

"They look just like the puppies in *So Many Puppies*," said Sammy.

"That's what I said!" Jack agreed.

"Hey, want to hear a joke?" Sammy asked. He didn't wait for an answer. "What do you call a five-day-old dog in Sweden?"

Jack thought for a second. "How should I know?" he asked.

"A puppy!" Sammy crowed. He cracked himself up.

Jack laughed, too, but he didn't really think it

was such a funny joke. "How about this one?" he asked. "Why did the dog carry a clock?"

Sammy shrugged.

"Because he wanted to be a watchdog!" Jack said. He laughed. He thought that one was much better.

"You guys should pay more attention to your puppies and less to your jokes," Lizzie suggested.

Jack made a face at her, but he knew she was right. Cocoa was about to crawl inside the pots-and-pans cabinet and Buddy was heading back to Skipper, probably for more food. Jack and Sammy helped round up all the puppies and get them into the box with Skipper.

After the Petersons – and Sammy – had finally eaten their pancakes, Mum said it was time to try giving the puppies their first real food. Ms Dobbins had told the Petersons how to do it. Mum mixed up some puppy formula with rice cereal, and Jack helped scrape the gooey mess into a special puppy-feeding dish Ms Dobbins had given them.

Lizzie spread newspapers on the kitchen floor, and Jack set the dish on the papers. The puppies waded right into the food as if it were a swimming pool on a hot day!

Yum, thought Cocoa. She stuck her face into the delicious-smelling mush and licked some up.

What is this? Cinnamon wondered. She nibbled some of the gooey stuff off Cocoa's ear.

Buddy knew the white stuff was food, but he couldn't figure out how to eat it. It was different from nursing. Oh, well. At least it smelled nice. It might be a good place for a nap.

Everybody laughed when Buddy laid down in the middle of the dish. Cinnamon jumped out and shook herself off, just like a grown-up dog. White goo flew everywhere! Then Cocoa walked out and trotted over to Jack, leaving a trail of sticky white footprints across the kitchen floor. Buddy just rolled around in the dish, as if he didn't know what to do with all that food.

Everybody laughed some more.

What a disaster! Jack could hardly believe that three tiny puppies could make such a gigantic mess.

Lizzie picked up Cinnamon and started to dry her off with a paper towel.

Sammy dived to catch Cocoa before she made even more footprints.

Mum tried to pull Buddy out of the dish and keep the Bean from getting into the dish. "This is ridiculous!" she said.

"Oh, well!" said Dad as he ran for more paper towels. "Puppies will be puppies!"

Chapter Six

Lizzie's best friend, Maria, showed up next. She arrived right in the middle of the puppy-food disaster.

"Wait! Let me get a picture before you clean them up!" Maria and Lizzie had talked on the phone about creating a poster with a picture of the puppies. Then they could put it up all over town. There had to be at least three people in Littleton who wanted puppies! It would be great to have new owners all lined up by the time the puppies were old enough to go to their forever homes.

Maria pulled her digital camera out of her backpack, knelt down, and started to snap picture after picture. *Flash!*

What was that bright light? Cocoa stared up at the new girl. Then she charged straight for her, tumbling over herself in her eagerness to check things out. She put her nose right up against the new girl's flashy thing. That made the new girl squeak!

Cinnamon sat down with a thump and started to clean herself, the way her mother had just begun to teach her. It wasn't as much fun as licking a person, but the goo all over her legs did taste pretty good.

Buddy was still hungry, but he couldn't get to his mum for milk. Not with the scary flashy thing in the room! He tried to hide behind Jack's knee. He knew he would be safe there.

Skipper got to her feet and wandered over to the dish the puppies had abandoned. She was extra hungry these days, since she was nursing. This stuff didn't look or smell like her usual food – but it was still food, so she might as well eat it! She began lapping the dish clean.

"Hey, Skipper, that food is for your puppies!" Lizzie said. "Oh, well."

Maria sat back on her heels, laughing at the puppies. "Wow, they really are cute," she said. "You guys are so lucky! They look just like the puppies in—"

"*So Many Puppies*!" chorused Lizzie and Sammy and Jack.

"They have names now," Lizzie said. She introduced Maria to all the puppies. "Cocoa is the adventurous one who almost put her nose on your camera. Cinnamon is the sweet one who's always trying to kiss you. And Buddy is the shy one behind Jack's leg."

"I love those names!" said Maria. "They're perfect. These *puppies* are perfect. You'll find homes for them in no time." She pulled Cinnamon on to her lap and let the puppy lick her cheek.

"I hope you're right," said Mrs Peterson with a sigh as she wiped puppy food off the front of the Bean's sweater.

Maria pushed the playback button on her camera and showed everybody the pictures she'd taken. The puppies looked adorable – but messy! The one of Cinnamon licking food off Cocoa's ear was everybody's favourite. It was hilarious.

"Maybe those aren't the best pictures for our sign," Lizzie said. "Let's finish cleaning up the pups and try again."

By the time the puppies were dry and clean, they were also very, very sleepy. That made it easy to pose them inside Lizzie's school backpack, with just their cute little heads and paws poking out. "Say 'Cheese!' No, say 'Puppy chow!'" said Maria as she snapped away.

When they were sure they had some good pictures, Lizzie and Maria put the puppies in the box next to Skipper for a nap. Then the girls headed upstairs and got to work on the poster.

Lizzie loved making posters on the computer. She had done it for some of the other puppies her family had fostered, so by now she was pretty good at it. First she and Maria uploaded the puppy pictures. It was hard to choose the cutest one! They were all adorable.

Then Lizzie typed a headline that read, "WE NEED GOOD HOMES!" Underneath, she put in all the information she knew about the puppies: their age, that there were two girls and a boy, and when they would be ready for adoption.

"Maybe you should put something about what kind of dogs they are," said Maria. "They look like they might be part husky or something, the way their ears stick up."

Lizzie glanced up at her "Dog Breeds of the World" poster. "Husky?" she said. "I never thought of that, but you might be right. For that matter, they might be part Saint Bernard, if you look at their colouring." She laughed. "They could be almost anything. But they'll grow up to be great dogs, just like their mum."

When the sign was finished, they brought it downstairs to show everybody.

"Aww," said Mum. "Very cute."

"Looks great," said Dad. "If you want to put some up downtown, I can give you a ride there and then you can walk back home. I'm headed to the fire station for a meeting."

Jack and Sammy promised to help Mum keep track of the puppies while Lizzie and Maria put up posters.

Dad dropped the girls off near the post office. They headed down the street, stopping in the shoe store, the dry cleaner's and the bakery. Everybody loved the poster and was happy to put it up, but nobody wanted a puppy. "Got three dogs at home already," grumbled the lady at the shoe store. "My son's allergic," said the owner of the dry cleaner's. "I don't think my cats would appreciate a puppy," said the girl behind the counter at the bakery.

Lizzie and Maria put up a poster in each shop. Then they kept walking down the block. "Hey, look at this!" Maria said, stopping at a bookstore window. "This would be the perfect place to put up a poster."

Lizzie read the name on the sign. "Lucky Dog Books," she said. "There's always been a bookstore here, but that's a new name."

"New owner, too," said a very tall, white-haired man who was putting some books on a display table in front of the store. "I just sold my bookshop in New York City so I could move to a smaller town. I love Littleton already!" He smiled at the girls. "I'm Jerry Small," he said. "I know, it's a funny name for someone my size. But I'm stuck with it. Just remember: Jerry Small is tall. Anyway, what do you have there?"

Lizzie showed him a poster. "Can we put this up in your window?" she asked.

He took one look and broke into a wide grin. "You sure can," he said. "Hey, those puppies look kind of familiar."

"Maybe it's because they look like the ones in *So Many Puppies*!" Maria suggested.

"That's what everybody says," Lizzie told him.

Jerry Small nodded. "That's it!" he said. "Maybe I'll put the book in the window, too. I'm trying to figure out good ways to get people to come into the shop. Nobody seems to know I'm here!"

He scratched his chin. "Didn't I hear that Mary Thompson just moved to Littleton? Maybe having a book by a local author in the window will help bring in business." He looked at the poster again. "Those puppies sure are cute," he said.

"They'll be ready to adopt in a couple of weeks," Maria said with a smile.

"Want us to save you one?" asked Lizzie hopefully.

"I'd love to have a puppy," Jerry said. "I've always had dogs. In fact, my store is named after my last one, Lucky." He looked sad for a moment. "Lucky was the best dog ever. He hung around my old bookshop with me. All the customers loved him. Lucky made me laugh every single day." He shook his head and smiled.

"But right now I have to concentrate on getting some customers into the shop," he went on. "Once I have enough business, maybe I can think about adopting a dog." Jerry took the poster and taped it to his window. He promised to show the girls some pictures of Lucky the next time they came to the shop.

Lizzie and Maria walked around town some more and put up the rest of the posters. When they had taped up the last one, Maria said she had to head home, so Lizzie walked home alone.

As she walked, Lizzie thought about how nobody they had talked to was ready to adopt a puppy. She was beginning to understand why Ms Dobbins was always so upset about all the unwanted puppies and dogs in the world. And she was beginning to see that it was going to be harder than she thought to find homes for three puppies – even if they *were* the three cutest puppies ever.

Chapter Seven

When Lizzie got home that afternoon, the house was quiet. She headed into the kitchen and found Mum sitting near the puppies' box, looking upset. "Oh, Lizzie!" she said. "I'm glad you're home."

"What's the matter?" Lizzie asked.

"I'm really worried about the little boy puppy," Mum said. "Buddy. He just doesn't seem – right." She and Lizzie looked into the box.

Sure enough, the tan puppy was curled up in a tiny ball, hardly seeming to notice the way his sisters stepped all over him as they played tug of war with Snakey. "I think he's shivering," said Lizzie. She had never seen a puppy tremble like that before. "Poor Buddy!" she said. "Where's Dad? Where's Jack?"

"Dad's not back yet, and Jack and Sammy just headed out to walk Rufus and Goldie," Mum said, biting her bottom lip. She really looked upset.

"Mum, we have to call the vet," Lizzie said. "Dr Gibson will know what to do."

Mum nodded seriously. "That's exactly what I was thinking," she agreed. "I guess I was waiting until Dad got home, so we could drive the puppy over to the animal hospital."

"I don't think we should wait any more," Lizzie said. Buddy looked really sick. He had hardly moved since she had started watching him, even though Skipper was nudging him with her nose. All he could do was lie there, shaking.

Buddy could feel his mum touching him, but he just wanted to be left alone. He was so tired! He was hungry, too, but he just didn't have the energy to fight his sisters over food any more.

Mum called Dr Gibson and told her all about Skipper and her puppies. Then she explained how Buddy didn't seem to have the same kind of pep that his sisters had. Lizzie sat watching Buddy while Mum talked. She was worried about him.

"Dr Gibson says she'll come right over," Mum reported when she got off the phone.

Ten minutes later, Dr Gibson rang the doorbell. "Let's see those puppies!" she said with a smile when Lizzie answered the door. Lizzie felt better right away.

"Oh, look," said Dr Gibson when she came into the kitchen. "Aren't they cute?" She squatted down by the box. "I see what you mean about this little guy," she said. She reached in and, very gently, picked Buddy up. She felt him all over and looked in his eyes, mouth and ears. "You'll be OK, sweetie," she said softly as she petted the tiny pup.

Buddy whined. Skipper, who was down at Dr Gibson's feet, whimpered, too. It was as if she were saying, "Can you help my baby?" Meanwhile, Cocoa and Cinnamon romped around Dr Gibson's trainers, attacking her shoelaces.

"It's exactly what I thought," said Dr Gibson. "I think he's just undernourished. That means," she went on when she saw Lizzie's puzzled look, "that he's not getting enough to eat. That sometimes happens to the smallest puppy. They call puppies like Buddy 'the runt of the litter'."

"We've noticed that he gets pushed out of the way a lot," Mum said. "So what do we do?"

Dr Gibson pulled a small bottle out of her bag. "We give him some extra puppy formula," she said. "That way, whether his sisters let him eat or not, we make sure he gets enough." She showed Mum and Lizzie how to put a few drops of puppy formula on to their fingers and teach Buddy to lap it up. Then they slowly guided him towards the tip of the bottle, so that he understood where to get more food. Finally, the doctor asked Lizzie to sit down and hold Buddy on her lap to feed him.

Soon the puppy was sucking away greedily, with

his eyes closed. Lizzie could almost see his soft tan belly getting rounder. "He sure was hungry," she said softly. She stroked the white heart on his chest.

"I think he'll perk up pretty soon," said Dr Gibson, "but you'll need to feed him as often as possible for a few days. That means a bottle every three or four hours. Can you handle it, or would you like me to take him to the animal hospital and care for him there?"

"We can do it!" Lizzie said. "I'll set my alarm clock and get up in the middle of the night."

"Oh, no you won't," said Mum. "Tomorrow's a school day."

"I'll stay home from school!" Lizzie said.

Mum was shaking her head. "I don't *think* so," she said. "Anyway, Mary Thompson is visiting Littleton Primary tomorrow, remember? You don't want to miss that." She looked up at Dr Gibson. "But Buddy will be fine here," she said. "I'll take good care of him."

"I'm sure you will," said Dr Gibson. "Just call me if you have any problems I'm always happy to help out with foster puppies. They need all the friends they can get."

Before she left, she knelt down to pat Skipper, Cocoa and Cinnamon. "It's a real shame," she said. "There are just too many unwanted puppies in the world. It's not easy to find homes for all of them." Dr. Gibson looked at Lizzie. "Well, you probably know all about that, working at the shelter."

Lizzie nodded. "Ms Dobbins has a sign up that says that if one dog has puppies, and *they* have puppies, and their puppies have puppies, you can end up with almost seventy *thousand* dogs in seven years!"

"Wow," Mum said. "That's a lot of puppies."

"And puppies grow up into dogs," said Lizzie. "You should see how many dogs there are at Caring Paws right now. And they all need homes."

"That's right," said Dr Gibson. "And any dog that found a home with caring people like you

54

would be a very lucky dog." She patted Skipper one more time and said goodbye. But what Dr Gibson said made Lizzie think. She was so busy thinking that she forgot to say goodbye back.

Lucky dog, Lizzie thought. *Just like the name of Jerry Small's bookshop.* Lizzie wanted to help more of the dogs at Caring Paws become lucky dogs, with families of their own. And she wanted to help Jerry Small get people to come to his store. If he had more business, he might even adopt one of the puppies. Jerry was such a nice man, and the bookstore would be a great home for a puppy.

Lizzie was beginning to get an idea of how to help the dogs at Caring Paws, Skipper's puppies, *and* Jerry – all at the same time!

Chapter Eight

"Buddy still looks kind of weak," Jack said the next morning at breakfast. "Maybe Lizzie and I should stay home from school and help take care of him." He looked over at the little tan puppy in his mother's lap. Buddy looked back at him with his soft brown eyes. Jack could almost *feel* Buddy begging for Jack and Lizzie to stay home. Cinnamon and Cocoa were fine on their own, but Buddy needed them.

Jack waited for Lizzie to say something, but she was just staring into her cereal bowl, deep in thought.

Sammy, who was finishing off his second piece of toast, instantly agreed. "I'll help, too," he said. Sammy also loved Buddy. Plus, he was always happy to skip school for a day.

"Thanks for the offer," said Mrs Peterson. "But the Bean and I can take care of Buddy just fine. I fed him twice in the middle of the night. He's already looking much better." She looked down at the tan puppy. "Aren't you, Mr Buddy?" she asked, in a baby-talk voice. Buddy reached up a paw when he heard his name, and Mum bent down to kiss him on the head.

Buddy loved this lady. She loved him, too, he could tell. He felt at home in her lap. It was almost as good as being curled up with his mother. He snuffled into her cheek when she kissed him.

Mum giggled.

She actually *giggled*! Jack looked over at Lizzie and raised his eyebrows, but Lizzie didn't seem to notice. Jack had never seen their mother act quite like that around a puppy. But Buddy could melt anybody's heart. There was just something special about him.

"Buddy!" yelled the Bean. He reached up to touch the puppy.

"Hey, cool! The Bean knows Buddy's name already!" said Jack. That was the first time the Bean had called any puppy by its real name. Usually he just said "uppy".

"Easy," Mum cautioned the Bean. "That's good," she said when the Bean gave Buddy a soft pat on the nose. "That's the way to pat a puppy."

"Pat me!" the Bean demanded. He toddled over to Jack and bumped his head up against Jack's knee. Jack patted his head gently. "Good Bean," he said. "That's a good Bean." The Bean laughed and went around the table getting pats. Pretending to be a dog was his favourite game.

After breakfast, Jack, Lizzie and Sammy gave the Bean and the puppies a few last pats and headed off to school. "What's up with you?" Jack asked his sister. "You're, like, out of it."

"Just thinking," Lizzie said. "I'm working on an idea." Then she started talking so fast that Jack could barely keep up. "See, I'm thinking about all the dogs at Caring Paws, and how they all need homes, and how our puppies are going to need homes, too. We need to get the word out."

Lizzie swung her bookbag as she talked, getting more and more excited. "And I was also thinking about that new bookstore. It's called Lucky Dog Books, and the owner is really, really nice. His name is Jerry Small, and he loves dogs. If he gets enough business, he might even adopt one of the puppies! But he needs people to know his store is there."

Jack and Sammy looked at each other. What was Lizzie getting at?

"So what I'm thinking is this," Lizzie continued. "What if there was a big grand-opening party at the bookstore – and we invited all the dogs from the shelter? People would come to the bookstore for the party, but they would also get to meet the dogs – and Skipper's puppies, too. And maybe some of them would get adopted! They would be lucky dogs, all right!"

Jack and Sammy were nodding. "It's a great idea," Jack said.

"It'll be a lot of work," Lizzie warned. "First I have to talk to Ms Dobbins and Mr Small," said Lizzie. "Maybe Maria and I can make cookies and punch..." She swung her bookbag some more. "But how can we make sure that lots and lots of people come to the store?"

All the way to school, Lizzie kept talking and Jack and Sammy just kept nodding. Lizzie was like that. Once she got an idea, she couldn't think or talk about anything else.

But once they got to school, Jack forgot all about Lizzie's idea. During morning meeting, Mr Mason reminded class 2B that it was "meet the author" day. Mary Thompson would be in the library, reading to each class in turn.

"I'd like you to think of some questions to ask her," Mr Mason told the class. "It's not every day that we get to talk to a real, live author." He had put some of Mary Thompson's books out on display.

Jack could hardly wait until it was his turn to share news. "Guess what came to stay with us this weekend?" he asked when Mr Mason called on him. He pointed to the copy of *So Many Puppies* Mr Mason had put out. "Puppies! And they look just like those."

He fumbled in his backpack and pulled out the sign Lizzie and Maria had made. "See?" he asked, passing it around. Everybody said, "Awww!" when they saw the puppies. Jack told about how the puppies had ended up at their house, and what their names and personalities were.

"Are they going to live with you for ever?" Mr Mason asked.

Jack shook his head. "No," he said sadly. "I wish we could keep one. But we're just fostering them. They all need good homes."

All morning, Jack kept glancing at the cover of *So Many Puppies*. He couldn't wait to hear Mary Thompson read it out loud. Finally, after lunch, it was his class's turn to go down to the library.

Mum was right: Mary Thompson didn't act like a famous person. She was short and round and cosy-looking, with grey hair and a bright red scarf around her neck. She sat on the floor and invited everybody to sit in a circle with her. Then she read two of her books out loud, showing the pictures and stopping to ask questions like, "Does anybody here have a younger brother or sister?" and "What kind of animal do you think Susie saw?"

Jack was sort of disappointed that she didn't read *So Many Puppies*. But he liked the books she did read.

Then it was question time.

"Where do you get your ideas?" asked Simon.

"How many books have you written?" asked Lucy.

"Do you draw the pictures in your books?" asked Robert.

"Do you like dinosaurs?" asked Sammy.

Mary Thompson answered all the questions. Then Mrs Devine, the librarian, said there was only time for one more. Jack raised his hand and

Mary Thompson called on him.

"Which book of yours is your favourite?" asked Jack. "My favourite is *So Many Puppies*." He was dying to tell Mary Thompson about Cocoa, Cinnamon and Buddy, but he knew there wasn't time.

"Oh, I love that one, too," said Mary Thompson. "I adore puppies, even though I haven't had one for many, many years. But I wrote that book a long time ago! Usually whatever book I'm working on right now is my favourite."

The bell rang just then, and Mr Mason told the class to thank Mary Thompson. Then it was time to go.

Jack waited until everybody else had left, then he went up to Mary Thompson. Just like Lizzie, he'd had an idea. He was almost too shy to ask, but the author seemed so nice. What did he have to lose?

He stood there for a minute, not sure what to say. Mary Thompson smiled at him and raised her eyebrows, like she was waiting for Jack to speak.

Jack smiled shyly back at her. "Would you like to come to a party?" he asked.

Chapter Nine

"Welcome to our party!" Lizzie said to a woman with a little boy.

Lizzie was greeting people at the bookstore door. "Would you like a balloon?" She handed the boy a red balloon with a picture of a dog on it. "There's cookies and punch in the children's section, and later on Mary Thompson will be reading and signing her books."

Lizzie's great idea had come to life! Three weeks' worth of planning had paid off. It was obvious already that the Lucky Dog party was going to be an event to remember.

Everybody had helped with the planning. Ms Dobbins and Julie from the shelter, Dr Gibson,

Jerry Small, and even Mary Thompson had been meeting at the Peterson house. They had worked out every detail of the party. Lizzie couldn't believe Jack had got the author to help out! Having Mary Thompson at the party was going to bring lots of people to the bookshop. And she was a lot of fun. When they had their meetings, Mary always wanted to get the business part out of the way first, so they could move on to playing with the puppies.

Buddy was getting stronger every day, and all the puppies were growing up fast. Cinnamon could already sit on command, and Cocoa was learning to walk on a leash. All three puppies were eating solid food. They were just about ready for adoption. Lizzie and Jack tried not to think about that too much.

Dad had been spending hours at the computer, making a mix CD for the party – he *loved* finding just the right songs for any occasion – and

Mum had got an article into the *Littleton News* about the event. "Publicity!" she had said. "That's the key."

It must have worked, because people had been streaming into Lucky Dog Books ever since the party had started. "You Ain't Nothin' But a Hound Dog" was blaring over the sound system. Lizzie and Maria were taking their turn as official greeters.

"Are you interested in adopting a puppy or a dog?" Maria asked the woman and the boy Lizzie had greeted. "If you adopt today, you get three free vet visits, plus a book about dog training and care."

"We'll definitely take a look," said the woman. She smiled down at her son. "Jasper has been wishing for a dog ever since he was two years old."

"I know exactly how he feels," said Lizzie, giving Jasper a big wink. "Have fun!"

Just then, Jack and Sammy came running over. "We just put up three more yellow stickers!" Jack said.

"Great news," Lizzie answered. "Our system is

really working well." She almost hated to admit it, but it was true. At the very first planning meeting, Ms Dobbins had said they could not have all of the dogs from the shelter at the bookstore. "Too crazy," she said. "They'll be barking, and running around, and stealing food. Nobody in their right mind would adopt a dog who was acting like that."

Lizzie was disappointed – until Julie came up with the greatest idea. "That poster you and your friend made for the puppies is terrific," she had said to Lizzie. "If you can make a poster for each dog from the shelter, we can put them up at the bookstore that day. People will get to see what the dogs look like and read about them."

"Great idea," Ms Dobbins had said. "But there's one big problem. There's no way we can let people adopt dogs just from a poster. They really have to meet the dogs."

"You're right," said Julie. "I've been thinking about that. I think I've come up with a fun idea. We can have three different stickers on the posters: one can say adopt me; another can say someone's interested in me; and the last one can say I've found a home. The shelter is only a five-minute walk from the bookshop. If people want to go and meet the dogs, they can."

Now the posters were up – Maria and Lizzie had made the best ones ever – and the party was in full swing.

So far, there were four red "I'M A LUCKY DOG! I'VE FOUND A HOME!" stickers on the posters hanging all around the bookstore. Those dogs were already adopted! Lizzie knew she was going to miss walking them at Caring Paws, but she was happy to know that they had found forever families.

Jack and Sammy offered to be greeters for a while, so Lizzie and Maria took a walk around the bookstore. There were people reading all the signs and looking at the books for sale, too. Dad's CD was playing "How Much Is That Doggie in the Window?"– which meant that the Bean was helping out at the DJ booth. That was his favourite song lately. Mum was roaming around with her reporter's notebook. Dr Gibson was handing out pamphlets about how to keep your dog healthy. Julie and Ms Dobbins were taking turns over at the animal shelter, introducing dogs to their possible new families.

"Cool!" said Lizzie, pointing to one of the posters. "Somebody's interested in Tigger!" There was a yellow "SOMEONE'S INTERESTED IN ME. TODAY MIGHT BE MY LUCKY DAY!" sticker on Tigger's picture.

"Great," said Maria. "Hey, let's go and visit the puppies."

Skipper and her pups were the only real dogs allowed at the party. Jerry Small had set up a pen for them in the corner near the bookstore's cash register. He and Mary Thompson were visiting the puppies when Lizzie and Maria walked up.

"Who's a little Cocoa Puff?" cooed Mary Thompson, reaching in to pet Cocoa.

"Hey there, Mr Buddy!" said Jerry, picking up the tan puppy. "You sure have grown," he added, holding the squirming puppy close. "You're a big boy now."

Cinnamon gave a short bark, asking for the same attention her brother and sister were getting.

Pick me up! Pick me up! Cinnamon wanted a hug.

Cocoa licked the nice lady's hand. Yummy!

Buddy felt safe in the big man's arms – but where was Lizzie? And Jack? And their mum? He missed them all.

Skipper watched her puppies proudly. They were growing up so well! It was good that they liked to be around people, since she couldn't take care of them for ever. Soon they would be on their own.

"Hey, what's this?" Maria asked.

Lizzie's face fell when she saw the red "I'VE FOUND A HOME!" stickers on the puppies' pen. "All the puppies have been adopted?" she blurted. "No!" Somehow, she had never expected this. She knew her family was only fostering the puppies, but she still wasn't prepared to see them go to their real homes.

"I thought you'd be glad," said Mary Thompson. "Glad for Cocoa and Cinnamon, and glad for me." She picked up Cinnamon and cuddled both puppies together, next to her smiling round face.

"You mean—?" Lizzie stared at her.

Mary Thompson nodded. "I'm taking both these girls," she said. "I fell in love with them. Plus, it's time to write a sequel to *So Many Puppies*. Everybody always tells me how much they love that book. Now Cocoa and Cinnamon can star in another story!"

"And I'm taking Buddy," said Jerry Small. "A place called Lucky Dog Books needs a dog. This little guy will grow up here and be my mascot."

"Wow," was all Lizzie could say. This was good news. No, it was *great* news. All three puppies had found excellent homes. So why did she feel like crying?

Chapter Ten

"I don't know why I feel so sad, when the party was so much fun," Mum said.

"I'm sad, too," said Jack.

"I know what you mean," said Dad.

"I sad!" said the Bean, with a loud wail.

Lizzie sniffed and wiped her eyes.

The Lucky Dog party was over and the Petersons were home alone for what seemed like the first time in weeks. The party had been a huge success. At least seven dogs had found homes!

The puppies had found homes, too.

Which was probably why the Petersons looked so miserable, even though they were pretending to celebrate with ginger ale and pizza.

They sat in the kitchen, watching all three

puppies romp around together for one of the last times. They would be going to their new homes in a few days. Today was Saturday. On Wednesday, the puppies would get one last check-up from Dr Gibson. "Unless something changes," she had told Lizzie, "the pups should be ready to go to their new homes that day."

The puppies were being as funny as always. Cocoa was nosing towards the puppy dish, ready to climb inside. Cinnamon walked right over her sister in search of the puppies' new favourite toy: a rubber chicken. Buddy let out a ferocious puppy growl as he pretended to fight for the chicken, tugging it away from Cinnamon. The boy puppy was still smaller than his sisters, but now he was strong and healthy.

Ooh, look! Cocoa found a crumb of hidden food. Yummy!

Cinnamon growled back at Buddy. Hey, give me that chicken!

No, it's mine! Buddy let his sister know that she couldn't have the chicken all to herself. She couldn't bully him around any more!

"Hey, you," Mum said to Buddy as she picked him up to give him a hug. "Leave your poor sister alone." She nuzzled her nose into Buddy's neck. Then Lizzie heard her sniff.

"Mum!" Lizzie said. "You're crying."

"Am not!" Mum answered. "Maybe I just became allergic to dogs."

But Lizzie and Jack knew the truth. Mum had fallen in love with all the puppies, just like they had. And of all the puppies, everyone in the Peterson family loved Buddy best. Maybe it was because he'd needed their help most of all. Maybe it was because he was so small and cute. Whatever it was, the Petersons were going to have a very, very hard time saying goodbye to Buddy.

*   *   *

74

Over the next few days, the Petersons spent as much time as they could with the puppies. Mum kept feeding Buddy by hand, even though he had finally got strong enough to push his sisters aside when he was hungry. Lizzie and Maria took dozens of pictures of the puppies for a scrapbook they were making. Dad brought home new puppy collars for each of them: red for Cinnamon, purple for Cocoa, green for Buddy. And Jack and Sammy played with the puppies for hours, trying to teach them manners for their new homes.

Wednesday arrived all too soon. After dinner, Dr Gibson was the first to arrive. She got right down on the kitchen floor and played with the puppies while she checked them over. "These are the healthiest pups I've ever seen!" she said after a few minutes. "Even the little guy is in great shape now." She took off her stethoscope. "I'd say they're ready to go," she said. "Looks like their mum thinks so, too."

It was true that Skipper had become less and

less patient with the puppies. She still cuddled with them when they were sleepy, but she didn't put up with their play-biting or baby growls. She let them know that she deserved respect, batting them away with her paw when they got too rough.

Jerry Small and Mary Thompson arrived next. "Where are those sweet girls?" Mary asked, coming into the kitchen. "Oh, you cuties! I can't wait to take you home." She sat down on the floor and pulled Cinnamon and Cocoa on to her lap.

Jerry Small looked uncomfortable. Lizzie wondered why he wasn't picking Buddy up. "Listen," he said to the Petersons. "I have good news and bad news."

"Well, tell us the good news first," said Dad.

"Business is booming," reported Jerry, with a big smile. "Lucky Dog Books has been incredibly busy all week. Our grand-opening party really did the trick. Now everyone knows I'm there."

"So what's the bad news?" asked Jack. He held

his breath. Could it really be what he *hoped* it would be?

"Well," said Jerry, "I guess the bad news is that I think the store is too busy for such a young puppy. I'm afraid that Buddy wouldn't get the attention he deserves."

"So – you're not going to have a dog at the shop after all?" Lizzie asked. She saw Jerry and Mary exchange a look.

"I'd still like to have a dog," Jerry said. "I was wondering if I could adopt Skipper. I think she'd love it at the store." He bent to pat Skipper's ears. "What do you think, girl? Want to come be a bookshop dog?"

Skipper thumped her tail.

"I think that means yes," said Dad. "That's wonderful news, Jerry. Of course Skipper needs a home, too. And I'm sure she would love to be a bookshop dog."

"But what about Buddy?" Jerry asked.

Now Lizzie saw her mother and father exchange

a look. She crossed her fingers. Mum gave a tiny nod.

"I think Buddy has already found a home," said Mum. "Right here with us." She went to scoop up the tan puppy and give him a hug. Dad put one arm around her shoulders and reached the other hand around to tickle Buddy under the chin.

Lizzie and Jack whooped.

"Finally, we have a puppy of our own!" yelled Jack.

"Buddy! Buddy! Buddy!" chanted the Bean, dancing around the kitchen.

"You're going to stay right here with us," Lizzie told Buddy. She reached out to touch the heart on his chest, smiling and crying at the same time.

Buddy looked from one happy face to the other. What was everybody so excited about? He had known it all along. He belonged here in this house, with this family. Buddy had found the perfect forever home.